MUTI'S NECKLACE

THE OLDEST STORY IN THE WORLD

by LOUISE HAWES

illustrated by REBECCA GUAY

HOUGHTON MIFFLIN COMPANY

BOSTON 2006

www.houghtonmifflinbooks.com

The text of this book is set in Vendome.
The illustrations are rendered in watercolor and acryla gouache on watercolor paper.

LIBRARY OF CONGRESS CATALOGING-IN-PUBLICATION DATA
Hawes, Louise.
Muti's necklace : the oldest story in the world / by Louise Hawes ;
illustrated by Rebecca Guay.
p. cm.
Summary: Muti treasures the necklace her father gave her so much that she risks the wrath
of Egypt's Pharaoh when it falls into the water. Based on an ancient Egyptian story.
ISBN 0-618-53583-7
[1. Necklaces—Fiction. 2. Egypt—History—To 332 B.C.—Fiction.]
I. Guay, Rebecca, ill.   II. Title.
PZ7.H3126Mu 2006
[E]—dc22
2004013199
ISBN-13: 978-0-618-53583-5

Printed in Singapore
TWP 10 9 8 7 6 5 4 3 2 1

For Lily, who will not be moved
—L.H.

For my mother. Through love, support, and level critique,
she gave me a priceless gift: confidence.
—R.G.

THOUSANDS OF YEARS AGO,

before there was an alphabet or pencils or paper to write stories on, there was a daughter of Egypt whose family loved her very much. When she was born, her father carved her a necklace made of turquoise, blue as a dragonfly's wing, and carnelian, red as the inside of a pomegranate.

The girl's name was Muti, and she wore her splendid necklace everywhere. When she was small, it hung down to her belly. She loved to feel the stones chunka-chunka against her skin when she ran into her father's arms. "I am fast as the wind," she cried.

"But I can hold the wind," her father said. He hugged her tight and kissed the top of her head.

Necklaces don't grow, but little girls do. As Muti got bigger and taller, her necklace reached only to her chest. When she played Hounds and Jackals with her brother, Ankhu, she would stare at its bright colors while she waited for him to move. "You are as slow as honey dripping from the pot," she told him.

The gems near her heart winked at Muti whenever she won the game, but Ankhu always turned the board over and chased after her. "Can honey run like this?" he asked.

Muti grew older and taller still. Her necklace no longer went chunka-chunka against her belly or winked at her from her chest. But she could feel it snug around her neck and see it reflected in the stream where she and her mother did their family's wash.

"Like this," Mama told her, dipping the clothes up and down, up and down in the water.

Muti plunged her laundry into the stream, too. "Like this?" she asked, giggling and splashing cool water at her mother. Mama always laughed and splashed right back.

When Muti was thirteen, she went to work for King Snefru, mighty Pharaoh of all Egypt. She missed her family, but life at the palace kept her busy night and day. The evenings were filled with feasting and parties, which meant hundreds of dishes and bowls to clean. And early each morning, Muti found a quiet spot to do the Royal Laundry. Kneeling by the water's edge, she watched Pharaoh's pleasure boat as it sailed slowly, slowly around the Royal Lake.

One day, as Pharaoh let a cool breeze fan him while his servants rowed the boat, he noticed Muti dipping his clothes up and down, up and down near the shore. "Look how strong and graceful she is." He pointed his Royal Finger at Muti. "Get me twenty more girls like that for my rowers," he commanded his ship's captain. "And this one shall lead the rest."

The captain bowed low before the king. "Your will be done, oh Wonder of the Nile and Beloved of the Gods," he said. But he went off muttering, "Young girls as oarsmen? What can Pharaoh be thinking!" For a long time, the captain trained Muti and the other serving girls to row, showing them how to pull their oars together so that the boat would move quickly and smoothly over the water.

Finally, the day came when Pharaoh seated himself on a lion throne in the shade of the canopy and watched Muti and the other serving girls climb onto his boat. Muti's hair was twisted into long, elegant braids and, of course, she wore her prized necklace for luck.

"Like this," Muti said. She picked up her oar. The other girls stood behind her and followed her as she dipped the oar into the water. When she swept it back and pulled it out again, all the girls did the same. Slowly, slowly, the king's boat sailed around the lake.

While she rowed, Muti watched the sparkling reflection of her necklace on the surface of the water. When a pair of plover flew near the boat and circled overhead, Muti looked up, then brushed a strand of hair from her eyes. The clasp of her necklace, which had held fast all these years, suddenly broke. The lovely red and blue gems tumbled into the lake.

"No!" Muti stopped rowing and reached down into the water.

Behind her, the other rowers stopped rowing, too. "What is wrong?" yelled the captain. He put his huge hands on his waist. "Why have we stopped?"

"Our leader is not rowing," the other serving girls told him. "So neither are we."

The angry captain walked to where Muti stood at the head of the line. "Why aren't you rowing?" he shouted. "You know that The King, May His Boundless Wisdom Guide Us Forever, will complain of the heat if we stop moving."

"I have lost my necklace in the lake," Muti told the captain. "It shines like no other."

Behind her, the rest of the rowers held their breath. "Be careful," one whispered. "Forget about the necklace. It is not worth your life."

The captain stared into the lake, then waved his hand in Muti's face. "Keep rowing," he ordered. "You have lost a trinket. The world is full of them." He leaned close to Muti, his brows lowered over his black eyes. "If you hope to see the sun tomorrow, do not anger The King Who Knows No Peer."

But Muti remembered her mother kneeling beside the stream, splashing water back at her. She folded her slim brown arms and refused to move.

When King Snefru grumbled about the heat, the captain sent for Muti. She bowed low before Pharaoh, whose headdress glittered with silver and gold.

"Why have we stopped?" Snefru demanded, his voice like thunder. "I ordered you to row around the lake."

"I have lost my necklace, Owner of Oxen and Cattle Past Counting," Muti told him. "I need to feel it against my skin."

All the serving girls gasped. "Did you hear that?" they asked one another. "Muti has talked back to the king."

"Foolish girl," said Pharaoh. "Keep rowing. I will replace your necklace with an even larger one. I will send for jewels from my richest mines."

But Muti shook her head. She remembered playing Hounds and Jackals with her brother. "No, thank you, Monarch of Ten Thousand Vineyards," she told the king. "I prefer my own necklace to any other. No matter how large."

The serving girls and even the captain shook with fear as the king's face darkened. His forehead began to perspire under the sparkling headdress. But Muti folded her slender arms and refused to move.

"Send for the Royal Magician!" bellowed the king.

When the Royal Magician climbed aboard, he pounded his jeweled staff so hard against the deck that the whole boat shook. "Oh Ruler Who Prospers and Prevails," he said, "tell me what is wrong."

"Magic Brother," Snefru told him, keeping his distance from the cobra wrapped around the wizard's staff, "this girl will not pick up her oar."

The magician shook his ringed finger at Muti. "You have stopped all the rowers from rowing. Why?"

"I have lost my necklace in the water," Muti said. "It is very precious to me."

The cobra spread its yellow hood, but the magician only laughed. "Is that all?" he asked. "Row on, silly child. I will cast a spell and make you a hundred necklaces, each more beautiful than the one you have lost."

But Muti thought of her father. She remembered his kisses on the top of her head. "No, thank you," she told the Royal Magician. "I prefer my own necklace to any other. No matter how beautiful."

The captain, the serving girls, and even Pharaoh could hardly believe their ears. Who dared to refuse the powerful magician? But Muti folded her arms and would not row.

The magician fumed and
fussed. The cobra spat and hissed.
But Muti did not move. The magician
scolded and scowled. The cobra swayed back
and forth. But Muti only stared into the glassy lake.

Finally, the mighty magician threw his hands up and turned his
gaze on the water. As he chanted magic words to the waves, the lake under the
boat began to sink lower and lower. Soon the water split in half and formed two
glistening walls on each side of the king's boat.

Pharaoh and his captain
and all the serving girls looked
around them in amazement. Instead
of lazy waves, they saw only the soggy,
muddy bottom of the lake. And there, winking at
Muti from the center of a clam bed, was the lost necklace.

Muti dashed from the boat and scrambled across the wet mud. She plucked up the necklace, holding it in both hands. For just a moment, she put the bright stones to her lips, then tucked them into the folds of her tunic and climbed back to her place on deck. She raised her oar and all the rowers behind her raised theirs.

The magician spoke another spell so that the water that had split in two rushed back underneath the boat. Muti lowered her oar. The rowers behind her lowered theirs. At last, Pharaoh's boat began to move slowly, slowly around the lake.

As it glided along, the boat passed a one-legged heron swallowing three fish at the same time and a family of blue turtles sunning themselves on a rock. But the king saw none of these wonders. Instead, he sat on his throne, eating figs and watching the rowers. Or rather, he watched one rower. When Muti raised her oar, Pharaoh raised his eyes. When Muti's oar dipped into the water, his Royal Glance followed her graceful stroke.

That night, stretched across his gilded bed, Snefru tried to sleep. But when the sun rose and peered into his bedchamber, he was still awake. The whole night long, thoughts of Muti had filled his Royal Head. Over and over, he had seen her shake her black braids and tell him that her necklace was like no other.

Finally,
Snefru sent
for Muti. "You are
beautiful and proud
and brave enough to be a
queen," he told her. "I prefer you
to any other. Come live with me
and help me rule all Egypt."
Muti bowed, but she did not
smile. "No, thank you, Potentate
Without Peer," she told the king.
"You must rule Egypt without me.
I am going home."
"Rash child!" he called after her.
"Why choose a thatch hut over a
scepter and throne?"
"Because, Oh Sovereign of Seven
Hundred Store Houses," Muti told him,
"I prefer my own life to any other, no matter how fine."
Then she turned her back on the marble palace and went straight
home to beat Ankhu at a game of Hounds and Jackals.

ABOUT THE STORY

This book is based on one of three "Tales of Wonder" in the Papyrus Westcar, a collection of the oldest written stories in the world. Because magicians were much more important in ancient Egypt than serving girls, the papyrus never mentions the name or the family of its plucky heroine, nor does it tell what happens to her after Snefru's magician divides the waters of the lake.

When I studied these tales in graduate school, I often marveled at the way the mighty kingdom of Egypt and the whole world of supernatural magic are dwarfed by the will of one small girl. So although the Egyptian tale ends with a detailed description of the great rewards the king heaps on his magician, I have given Muti not only a name and a history, but her Pharaoh's admiration as well. I think that's the very least such a stout heart deserves!